THE RISE AND FALL
OF THE KATE EMPIRE

Adapted by Kirsten Larsen
Based on the series created by Terri Minsky
Part One is based on a teleplay written
by Nina G. Bargiel and Jeremy J. Bargiel.
Part Two is based on a teleplay written
by Alison Taylor.

DISNEY CHANNEL SM

DISNEY PRESS

New York

Printed in the United States of America

First Edition
1 3 5 7 9 10 8 6 4 2

Library of Congress Catalog Card Number: 2002093173

ISBN 0-7868-4541-4
For more Disney Press fun, visit www.disneybooks.com
Visit ZoogDisney.com

Lizzie McGuire

PART ONE

CHAPTER ONE

Lunch tray in hand, Lizzie McGuire stood before the crowded outdoor courtyard at Hillridge Junior High, searching for a table. Lunch tables. They were claimed, named, and declared group turf the first day of each school year. There was the math club table, the skate rat table, even a table for the future misfits of America. But what really irked Lizzie was the cheerleaders' table. Theirs was the very table Lizzie and her best friends,

Gordo and Miranda, had claimed for themselves at the beginning of the school year—only to have the cheerleaders reclaim it for *themselves* the next day. Ever since, finding seats for herself and her friends was a major pain. And today, Lizzie's patience was thinned by hunger. All she wanted to do was plop down and devour her cafeteria special. Was this too much to ask? Couldn't everyone just get along? At least long enough to scarf down a plate of mac and cheese? Lizzie blew a strand of blond hair out of her eyes and searched around some more.

"I don't see any seats," Miranda said with a sigh, holding a tray with a now chilled slice of pizza and a carton of orange juice on it. Gordo joined them, holding his mom's specially prepared sushi rolls in a paper bag. They had to find three seats together; otherwise they'd be stuck sitting on the muddy grass again.

"There's three over there," Gordo said excitedly. Lizzie and Miranda took a step toward the place where he was pointing and then stopped. It was the cheerleaders' table.

Lizzie looked at Gordo, waiting for the punch line. But it appeared he wasn't kidding. "Gordo, we can't sit there," she said.

The cheerleading table is like the Oscars! You only go if you're nominated.

"Why not?" Gordo asked in a logical tone, as if logic had anything to do with it. "It's lunchtime. And I'm not eating bologna in the grass. Again."

"Yeah! We should take a stand and take

those seats back!" Miranda chimed in. Lizzie raised her eyebrows in surprise. Normally, Miranda was the first to obey the social hierarchy of junior high. But there she stood, holding her tray out like a soldier ready for battle. "Gordo?" Miranda said.

"It's time to draw a line in the sand," he declared. They both looked at Lizzie.

Sand? i don't even like the beach.

Lizzie looked at the cheerleaders. They're just people, she tried to reason. Beneath the pom-poms, there must be hearts. "Okay," Lizzie said nervously. "After you, Gordo." Together they all marched over to the cheerleaders' table, with Gordo leading the way.

Kate Sanders, captain of the cheerleading

squad and self-proclaimed queen of Hillridge Junior High, sat at the head of the table, spooning yogurt out of a little plastic container. Watching her, Lizzie thought how much Kate had changed. In grade school, Kate was actually nice and one of Lizzie's best friends. But then came junior high and Kate became a cheerleader. From that moment on, Kate mocked Lizzie relentlessly for her non-cheerleader/nonpopular status. It was like Kate had traded her soul for a pleated skirt.

Sitting next to Kate was her new best friend, Claire. Claire was the squad's stuck-up junior captain who seemed to enjoy mocking all the school "losers" even more than Kate did. As Gordo, Lizzie, and Miranda approached, Kate and Claire looked them up and down, their glossy mouths open in total disbelief.

"Um, Gordo, are you and your friends a bit

confused?" Kate asked. "This is a cheerleading-only zone."

"Buh-bye." Claire sneered as she waved the trio away.

But Gordo wasn't in the mood for pom-pom girls with a superiority complex. "You know, the cheerleading act is wearing a little thin," he snapped. "It's time things changed around here. Cheerleaders and noncheerleaders can sit down and eat at the same table." With each word, Gordo's voice rose until he was almost shouting.

Suddenly, Gordo slammed his lunch tray down on the table with a loud smack. Kate and Claire jumped. It was one of the coolest things Lizzie and Miranda had ever seen.

"I'm stayin'. I'm finishing my lunch here," Gordo announced. He folded his arms across his chest and stared at Kate and Claire, as if daring them to make a move.

The two cheerleaders blinked at him, startled. Then they turned to each other and smiled.

Moments later, Gordo, Lizzie, and Miranda found themselves sitting on the wet muddy grass between two tables.

"It's not that I dislike Kate," Gordo said, glaring at the queen of all things evil. "It's just that I hate everything she represents."

"Yeah," Lizzie agreed. "I just wish one time she would know what it feels like to sit in the grass."

"It feels scratchy," Miranda said. Then, feeling the damp seat of her new plaid pants, "And wet," she added with a tight grin.

Suddenly, a loud shout boomed out across the quad, startling them all. "Gimme an *H*!" Lizzie turned to see the cheerleaders practicing their routine right behind them on the grass.

"Great," Lizzie snapped. "It's not bad enough we have to eat in the grass—now we have to watch them?"

"This is cruel and unusual punishment," Gordo said. "There are rules about this in the Constitution."

Miranda looked at him. There were? Gordo knew the strangest things. "Where does the Constitution stand on wet pants?"

But just as Gordo was about to answer, the loud cries of the cheerleaders' cheering drowned him out. There was nothing Lizzie, Miranda, and Gordo could do but watch Kate rustle her pom-poms and toss her long, perfect blond hair. She looked like she was born to do this. Lizzie scanned the courtyard and realized that everyone was awestruck by Kate's performance.

"Why is it that Kate always gets what she wants?" Lizzie asked with frustration.

"Because it's her world and we all just live in it?" Miranda suggested.

"I have everything I want," Gordo said—"except a seat. I hate picking ants out of my cheesy puffs." He shot an ant off his puff, then popped it into his mouth.

The cheerleading squad finished their rahrahs and were now ready for their big finale. This was their specialty—the big crowd-pleasing pyramid. Five girls kneeled on their hands and knees, three more girls jumped on their backs and then kicked up one foot. Now it was all about Kate. Eyeing her target, Kate ran, sprang, and then landed gracefully on top of the triangle of bodies. Kate was standing twelve feet above everyone else and she was beaming. She shot her hands up high in the sky.

Watching Kate, Lizzie frowned. "I wish that just once someone would come along and knock Kate right off her pedestal," she said.

Where's that big gust of wind when you need it?

Just then, a look of uncertainty flashed across Kate's face. Her legs began to wobble. She flapped her arms in the air, trying to regain her balance, but it was too late. With a piercing squeal, Kate pitched off the top of the pyramid and landed with a loud thud on the grass.

Miranda's and Gordo's mouths fell open. They turned and looked at a stunned Lizzie. "How'd you do that?" Miranda asked.

Since when do i control the wind?

The toppled cheerleaders climbed to their feet, laughing and dusting off their skirts. All except Kate. Kate wasn't moving. She was still lying in the grass where she had fallen. One of the girls reached out her hand to pull Kate up, but she groaned loudly and slapped the hand away.

"Well, I guess cheerleading practice is over," Gordo said cheerfully.

Lizzie winced. "Oh, that can't be good," she said.

CHAPTER TWO

The next day at lunch, Lizzie and her friends ran to the quad, determined to find actual seats at an actual table.

"There's one!" Gordo cried, pointing to a small table right in the middle of the quad. Lizzie, Miranda, and Gordo dashed over and swung their trays onto the table just seconds before a group of glee club kids reached it.

"Phew!" Lizzie said, settling herself into a chair.

"So, the word is, Kate dislocated her shoulder," Miranda reported, as she unwrapped her sandwich. All morning at school, everyone had been talking about the same thing: Kate Sanders's big fall.

"That'll take her out of cheerleading for a month," Gordo said. He glanced at Lizzie and added, "Thanks to Sabrina the Teenage Witch."

"I didn't do it," Lizzie protested. "I didn't want her to fall."

"We *all* wanted her to fall," Miranda corrected her.

"Yeah, but I didn't want her to get hurt." It was a small but important distinction, Lizzie thought.

"Well, that's the price you pay for having your wishes come true," Gordo told her.

At that moment, Kate entered the quad. She wore a blue cardigan sweater with a fake-fur collar draped over her shoulders. Beneath it, her left arm hung in a blue sling that she'd tried to disguise with a printed silk scarf. Even injured, Kate was seriously fashion conscious. But she was having a hard time balancing her tray with only one good arm. Awkwardly, she made her way through the crowded lunch area over to the cheerleaders' table and sat down.

"Ugh," Kate groaned dramatically. "It took me forty-five minutes to get dressed this morning. This sling does not accessorize well."

But there was no response from her minions. The other cheerleaders kept quiet and glanced nervously over at her.

Kate looked around at them. "What?" she asked.

Suddenly, Claire stood up. Taking a deep breath, she looked Kate in the eye and said, "Kate, this is the cheerleaders' table."

"And I'm a cheerleader," Kate told her, annoyed.

The other cheerleaders looked away. Claire smiled at Kate pityingly.

"No, you're not," she said. "You can't be a cheerleader with a dislocated shoulder. Which means you can't be cheerleading captain. We took a vote. You're out."

Kate's blue eyes widened in astonishment. "I'm not out!" she cried. "You can't just do that!"

"Yes, I can," Claire said icily. "Because I'm the new cheerleading captain. Turn in your pom-poms after school." Then Claire leaned over and whispered loudly, "It'll be less embarrassing that way."

Kate's brow wrinkled in confusion. She looked around the table, but none of the other cheerleaders would meet her eye.

"I think you should leave now," Claire said smugly.

Kate stood and gripped her tray clumsily. The cheerleaders sitting nearest to her scooted away, as if they thought her new unpopularity might be contagious. Kate took one final look at her squad, then looked around the courtyard. She was searching the crowd for a friendly face—someone who'd invite her to sit with them—but all the kids looked down at their food, pretending to be busy eating. She had shunned every one of them in the past, so no one was feeling too badly about her predicament now. Embarrassed, Kate carried her tray over to an empty patch of grass.

"Wow," Lizzie said. She looked at Kate, then back to the cheerleading table, where the other girls had returned to chatting as if nothing had happened. "That was harsh."

Miranda grinned. "That was cool!"

"I wish I had my camera," Gordo said enthusiastically. "I mean, you hear about this stuff happening, but you never actually see it!"

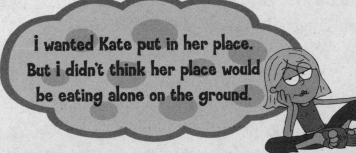

i wanted Kate put in her place. But i didn't think her place would be eating alone on the ground.

Lizzie couldn't help but glance over at Kate. "Guys, look at her," Lizzie said as she nudged her friends.

They turned in their seats to watch the fallen cheerleader. She was kneeling awkwardly in the damp grass, trying to peel the cellophane off her sandwich with one hand.

"She's all by herself. Maybe we should ask her to sit with us," Lizzie suggested.

"Hmm," Gordo said thoughtfully. "Should we ask her to sit with us? Miranda?"

Miranda pursed her lips, as if considering the question. Then she grinned. Simultaneously, Gordo and Miranda burst out singing, *"Dingdong, the witch is dead!"*

"Which old witch?" asked Gordo.

"The wicked witch!" Miranda chirped.

Lizzie stared at them "I'll take that as a no," she said dryly.

"Dingdong, the wicked witch is deaaaaaad!" sang Miranda and Gordo, happy as munchkins.

As they continued to sing, Lizzie glanced back over her shoulder at Kate, who was still kneeling in the grass. Alone.

Later that afternoon at the McGuire house, Lizzie's father and mother were in the kitchen, cooking dinner, when the back door opened. In walked Lanny, their son Matt's silent best friend. Matt's parents never succeeded in getting Lanny to speak, but this just made them all the more determined.

"Hi, Lanny," Mrs. McGuire said, smiling anxiously.

Lanny looked at Mrs. McGuire and smiled.

Mr. McGuire glanced up from the onions he was chopping. "Where's Matt?" he asked.

Lanny's smile turned mysterious as he glanced to the right. Then he looked to the left, and threw out his arms, gesturing toward the back door. Suddenly, the door flew open and Matt strode into the room. He folded his arms across his chest and looked haughtily at his parents.

"Hi, Matt," said Mrs. McGuire.

"How was school today?" Mr. McGuire asked.

"School? How was school?" Matt boomed. He flared his nostrils and sucked air through his teeth. "School was . . . fantastic!"

Mrs. McGuire looked at him curiously. "Are you okay?" she asked.

"I think his voice is changing," Mr. McGuire said, turning back to the onions.

Matt sighed impatiently. "My voice *is* changing," he told his parents. "It's becoming *theatrical.*"

Matt's parents stared at him blankly.

"You're looking at the star of the school play," Matt explained.

Lanny looked at Matt and cocked an eyebrow. The *star*?

"Okay, it's only one line," Matt admitted. "But what a line!"

"Congratulations, honey! That's wonderful," Mrs. McGuire exclaimed. She clapped her hands proudly. "My son, the actor."

Mr. McGuire put down the chopping knife and wiped his hands on the apron he was wearing. "I knew you could do it!" he told Matt.

His wife glanced at him, "You knew he was

trying out for the play?" she asked out of the corner of her mouth.

"Not a clue," Mr. McGuire muttered back, then added in a loud whisper. "It's called 'acting.'" Mrs. McGuire smiled and rolled her eyes.

"My part holds the entire play together," Matt informed them. Lanny frowned and shook his head.

"Lanny, there are no small parts, only small actors!" Matt exclaimed. He looked at his parents and, with a sweeping gesture, cried, "Exit! Stage left!"

Lanny grabbed the hood of Matt's sweatshirt and pulled him back. He jerked his thumb in the opposite direction.

"Thanks, Lanny," Matt said. "You're a good understudy." With another arm flourish, he cried, "Exit! Stage right!" As Mr. and Mrs. McGuire watched, Matt and Lanny swept out of the room.

CHAPTER THREE

"**D**id you finish the homework?" Gordo asked the next morning as he, Lizzie, and Miranda headed up the stairs to algebra class.

"I finished it," Lizzie replied, shifting her math book to her left arm. "But that doesn't mean I understood it."

Rounding the corner to Mrs. Wortman's classroom, they spotted Claire strutting toward them from the opposite direction, leading a posse of cheerleaders. Claire's eyes narrowed as she caught sight of them. As the two groups met in the middle of the hallway, Claire stopped and placed her hands on her hips. "Excuse me," she said. "I believe you're in the wrong place." The other cheerleaders smirked.

"What do you mean?" Lizzie asked. She glanced at Miranda and Gordo to see if they knew what Claire was talking about. They shrugged.

"We're just going to math," Miranda told Claire.

"Well, you'll have to find another way to go. This is a cheerleaders-only hallway," she replied. "The 'dork' hallway is down in the basement."

Lizzie, Miranda, and Gordo stared at her in astonishment.

"You have got to be joking," Miranda said.

"That's ridiculous," Gordo told Claire. "Our classroom is right there." He pointed to a door just behind Claire.

Claire arched her eyebrows. Saying nothing, she lifted her arm and pointed one frosted pink fingernail down the hallway, ordering Lizzie and her friends back the way they had come. With the other cheerleaders firmly blocking their path, the trio had no choice but to turn around, take the west stairs down to the basement, walk all the way down the second-floor corridor, and go back up the east stairs.

As the day went on, the cheerleader situation only got worse. At lunch, Claire not only banned noncheerleaders from the cheerleaders' table, she banned them from *all* the tables! As Claire and the other cheerleaders spread out and lounged upon the lunch tables, everyone else was forced to sit on the ground. The grass was so packed with students that Lizzie and her friends could barely walk through the quad.

"I hate this," Lizzie said as she stumbled over someone's thermos, looking for a place to sit. "Claire is ten times worse than Kate."

"I know," Miranda said. "It's like Kate, the Sequel."

At last, Lizzie and her friends found a tiny space in the grass. They squeezed between some other kids, holding their trays on their laps to make more room.

"Did you hear what Claire did to Jennie Woods?" Lizzie asked, lowering her voice. Miranda nodded.

"What'd she do?" Gordo asked.

"Jennie was wearing the same outfit as Claire today. So Claire made her wear her gym uniform for the rest of the day," Miranda informed him. Gordo wasn't properly horrified, but then again, Gordo wasn't a fashion-conscious girl.

"She's out of control," Lizzie said, shaking her head.

"I know. I mean, look at us!" Gordo cried. "We're eating lunch on the grass! At least with

Kate we had a chance at getting a table! But now we're doomed to the grass. It doesn't get any worse than this!"

"At least if you stayed out of Kate's way, she'd leave you alone," Lizzie pointed out.

"Claire seems to enjoy her work," Miranda said.

Gordo nodded. "I guess the enemy you know is better than the one you don't."

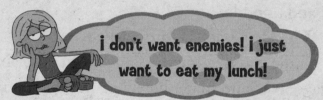

i don't want enemies! i just want to eat my lunch!

After school that afternoon, Mrs. McGuire came into the living room as Lanny was helping Matt rehearse his big scene for the school play.

"Ah! The doorbell!" Matt bellowed. "I'll get that!"

His mother looked bewildered. "I didn't hear the doorbell," she said.

Matt glanced at Lanny and rolled his eyes. "Of course not," he said. "I was acting."

Mrs. McGuire looked confused.

"It's my line. For the *play*," Matt explained. "You see, the motivation for my character is that someone is *at* the door, and I must answer it. If I don't, the play shuts down completely."

"O-kay," Mrs. McGuire replied slowly. "I'll bring you guys some snacks."

As she left for the kitchen, Matt clapped his hands together. "Okay, Lanny, from the top!"

Lanny nodded and picked up a pen and a glass of water from the table. Gently, he tapped the pen against the rim of the glass. *Ding!*

"Ahhhhhhh . . . the doorbell? I'll get that?" Matt said, his voice rising in a question.

Lanny shook his head and tapped the glass again. *Ding!*

"Ah-the-doorbell-I'll-get-that!" Matt shouted.

Lanny shrugged. Better, but still not great.

He tapped the glass a third time. *Ding!*

"Ah!" Matt exclaimed. "The doorbell! *I'll* get that." This time Lanny smiled and clapped approvingly.

Just then, Mrs. McGuire returned from the kitchen. She placed a large bowl on the table.

"Mom! You're disturbing the process!" Matt shouted. Then he glanced into the bowl. "Ooooh! Trail mix!" He reached a hand into the bowl. *"Chocolate?"* he said.

Mrs. McGuire smiled. "Yes, I put extra chocolate chips in the trail mix. Just how you like it."

Lanny slapped his hand to the side of his head.

Matt snorted with disgust. "Mom, do you *know* what chocolate can do to a complexion? Take it away!" he commanded.

"Excuse me?" his mother said.

"Just bring it back when you've picked out all of the chocolate chips," Matt told her.

"I am not picking out the chocolate chips,"

Mrs. McGuire said, giving him a warning look.

"Fine. Then perhaps you could cut up some fresh papaya and bring that along with some green tea and honey," Matt suggested.

"I'm going to act like I didn't hear that," Mrs. McGuire snapped. "If you guys get hungry, the trail mix will be in the kitchen." She scooped up the bowl and left the room, muttering, "Actors."

Matt shook his head. "Mothers," he muttered. He turned to Lanny. "Okay, let's do our facial exercises. Lion face!" The two boys opened their eyes wide and bared their teeth, making a ferocious face.

"Lemon face!" Matt shouted. Quickly they pursed their lips and squeezed their eyes closed, as if sucking on a sour piece of lemon.

"Lion face!"

"Lemon face!" They made the sour face.

"Lion face!"

"Lemon face!"

CHAPTER FOUR

The next morning, Lizzie was walking down the crowded "dork" hallway on her way to math class, when she spotted Kate struggling to hold a pile of books in her good arm.

Kate? in the dork hallway? it's like i'm in another dimension!

As Lizzie watched, one of the books slipped from Kate's grasp and fell to the floor. Stepping over to her, Lizzie picked up the book and held it out. "Here," she said gently. "You dropped this."

"I've got it," Kate said curtly, trying to rebalance the other books in her arm.

"Why don't you have one of your friends help you?" Lizzie asked.

"Because I just don't, okay?" Kate answered. She kept her eyes turned away, pretending to be very interested in something extremely important going on down the corridor.

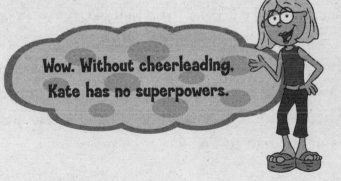

Wow. Without cheerleading, Kate has no superpowers.

"I'm really sorry about your shoulder," Lizzie tried again.

"It's fine," Kate snapped.

What are these strange feelings i'm having? i'm feeling sorry for Kate!

"And what happened in the lunchroom yesterday with Claire," Lizzie added quietly.

"Listen, I'm fine, okay?" Kate cried in frustration. Tears welled in her eyes. "I don't need help from you. Or anybody! Just leave me alone!" Snatching her book away from Lizzie, she stormed off down the hallway.

That girl needs some serious help, Lizzie thought. She watched Kate solo it down the hallway and fumble her books once more. Then suddenly, it hit her. Lizzie knew just what she had to do.

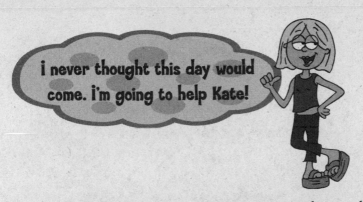

i never thought this day would come. i'm going to help Kate!

Later that afternoon, Lizzie, Miranda, and Gordo sat on the deck in the McGuires' backyard, sipping lemonade in the sunshine and going over their history homework. They were studying Cleopatra, the Egyptian queen.

"So, Cleopatra was betrayed by her best friend," Lizzie read from their textbook.

Miranda snorted. "Hmmm, that sounds familiar," she said.

"I think I'd rather face an asp than Claire at the cheerleading table," Gordo added.

Miranda quickly looked up the word "asp," then nodded in agreement.

I'm sure Claire would be more comfortable eating lunch with a snake.

"Yeah." Miranda jiggled the ice cubes in her glass. "But Kate totally deserves everything she's getting," she said firmly.

Lizzie looked at her. "She deserves it? Don't you think you're being a little harsh?"

"No. Lizzie, this is the girl who made up a nasty cheer about you in front of the whole school," Miranda reminded her.

"And she made our lives miserable," Gordo added. He rubbed his hands together. "It's payback time."

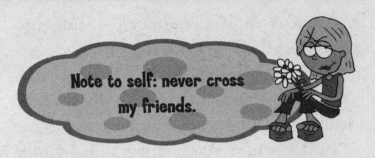

Note to self: never cross
my friends.

"Okay, so she's been kinda mean," Lizzie admitted.

Miranda stared at her. "Kinda?"

"But today I ran into her in the hallway," Lizzie told them. "Guys, if you could've seen her, you'd change your mind."

Miranda shook her head. "I don't think so."

"Me, neither. I don't know if I could hate her even more," Gordo said. Miranda giggled.

"Guys, seriously," Lizzie hesitated slightly—she knew what she was about to say would not go over well, but she had to say it. "I feel sorry for her."

Miranda's smile disappeared. Gordo pretended to fall off his deck chair in shock.

"I know it sounds crazy," Lizzie continued. "But without cheerleading, Kate has no friends."

"I think you're exaggerating a bit," Gordo said.

"Yeah, Kate has other friends," said Miranda.

Lizzie raised her eyebrows. "Like who?"

Miranda and Gordo thought for a moment.

"Wow," Miranda said at last, realizing she couldn't think of a single name.

"I never thought of it that way," Gordo said.

"I mean, I know that whatever happens, you guys will always be my friends," Lizzie said. "But Kate doesn't have anyone like you. She sits alone at lunch."

"We used to be friends with Kate,"

Miranda said. "There might be a human lurking under there somewhere." But Miranda looked doubtful as she said it.

Gordo shook his head. "I don't care what you guys are doing—I'm not gonna be friends with Kate."

"I was thinking more along the line of helping her out," Lizzie said.

"How?" Miranda asked.

"By making her popular again."

"Again?" Miranda looked at her in disbelief. "We can't make *ourselves* popular in the first place," she pointed out.

"It's an interesting idea," Gordo said. He tapped his pencil against his book thoughtfully. "And she's got to be better than Claire. I don't think I can stand another lunch with the huddled masses." He stood up from his chair and slapped his hand down on the patio table. "I'll do it."

Miranda glanced at Gordo and Lizzie.

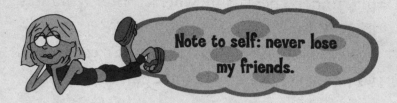

Note to self: never lose my friends.

Lizzie grinned. "So," she said, looking from Gordo to Miranda, "the question is—how do we help Kate without Kate's help?" Gordo looked skyward. Miranda doodled in her notebook. Lizzie's smile faded, and she bit her pencil. This wasn't going to be easy.

CHAPTER FIVE

Matt reclined on the couch in the McGuires' living room, holding a cell phone to his ear. He wore a pair of sunglasses and a silk scarf wrapped loosely around his neck. His normally spiky brown hair was stiff with extra hair gel. As he spoke, he held a compact mirror at arm's length and examined his reflection.

"Lanny, can't you do anything about this overhead lighting?" Matt whined into the phone. "It makes me look old!" He listened for a moment. "Fine," he said, snapping the compact shut. "Be that way." Holding the phone away from his ear, he screamed, "Moooooom! I need help! Now!"

Mrs. McGuire rushed into the living room. "What's wrong?" she asked, startled.

Matt casually glanced up at her. "Can you turn the lights down?" Without waiting for a reply, he said, "Thanks, you're a doll," and turned his attention back to the cell phone.

Mrs. McGuire stared at her son in disbelief. "You called me in here to turn the lights down for you?" she asked angrily.

"Uh-huh. They were aging me. Tell her, Lanny," he said into the phone.

Mrs. McGuire looked at Lanny, who was sitting at the other end of the couch. Lanny nodded briefly, then lifted a hand and coolly examined his fingernails. Mrs. McGuire turned back to Matt.

"Matt, I am you mother, not your flunky. Keep it up and you're gonna be grounded," she said. "And I told you to stop playing with the cell phones." She grabbed the phones out of Matt's and Lanny's hands and stormed out of the room.

Matt fell back against the pillows and heaved a sigh. "It's so hard to get good help these days," he said. "Lanny, turn down the lights."

Lanny cocked an eyebrow at Matt. *Excuse me?*

"Lanny, we're a team," Matt said impatiently. "I perform, and you help me."

Lanny narrowed his eyes accusingly.

"That's not what I mean, Lanny," Matt said.

Lanny shook his head sadly.

"I haven't changed, Lanny. *You've* changed!" Matt shouted.

Lanny stared blankly at Matt. He didn't have anything more to say to him.

"Fine," Matt snapped. "Forget it! Just leave then!"

Lanny stood up. With a proud flick of his head, he turned and stomped out the door.

Alone on the couch, Matt picked up the mirror and gazed at his reflection. "Ah. The doorbell," he said sadly. He sniffled slightly and wiped a tear from his eye. "I'll get that."

CHAPTER SIX

The next day at school, Lizzie could barely contain herself, she was so excited. Kate was on her way back, Claire was on her way down, and it was all because of Lizzie's genius plan.

"Gordo, this is brilliant," Lizzie said, as they took their seats in science class. "The buzz around Kate is huge."

"So, how's it going?" Gordo asked.

"Well, this morning I told Parker Kinney

in Social Studies, and by English, I had Jennie Woods telling *me* about Kate's aunt," Miranda reported.

"It's great," Lizzie said, glancing back at Kate who was seated in the back of the room. "Everyone totally believes that Kate's aunt was a Laker Girl."

Just then, Claire sauntered into the classroom, followed by two of her minions. They walked straight over to Kate.

Gordo nodded at them. "Looks like our plan's about to be put to the test," he remarked.

There may be rough waters ahead, but this plan is unsinkable!

"Kate, I heard about your famous cheer-leading aunt," Claire said, loud enough for the whole classroom to hear. "What an amazing coincidence that she suddenly appears when you've suddenly *disappeared* from the social world."

Kate's face turned red. "Listen," she said quickly, "I didn't start that rumor—"

"*Of course*, you didn't," Claire said sarcastically. "I'm sure it's part of some elaborate scheme to make you popular again—*not!*" The other cheerleaders giggled. Kate looked mortified.

I can't believe the plan didn't work, Lizzie thought. It seemed like it was unsinkable.

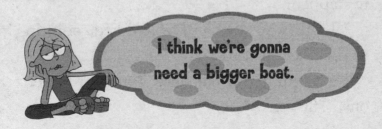

i think we're gonna need a bigger boat.

"It's really pathetic, Kate," Claire told her. "Take some advice from a former friend. Give it up." Tossing her long mane of curly hair, she walked away. The other cheerleaders trailed after her. Lizzie watched as Kate slumped down miserably in her seat.

"So," Lizzie said, turning to Miranda and Gordo, "what's plan B?"

At lunch that afternoon, Lizzie, Miranda, and Gordo spotted Kate sitting alone in a corner of the quad, picking at a salad. Lizzie couldn't take it anymore. She picked up her tray and headed right toward her. Gordo and Miranda followed, not quite knowing what was about to happen.

"Is this seat taken?" Lizzie asked, pointing to the grass next to Kate.

Kate squinted up at her. "You can't be serious," she said.

"I can't believe it myself," Gordo said, "but here we are."

"So scooch over, Sanders," Miranda added. Kate scooted over to make room. They set their trays down and began to eat. For a moment, everyone chewed in uncomfortable silence.

Lizzie couldn't hold it in any longer. She had to come clean. "I'm sorry about the rumor," she blurted out.

Kate groaned. "You guys started that rumor? Thanks for making my life even more miserable."

"We thought it would help," Miranda told her.

"Help what? Help Claire?" Kate snapped.

"Actually, Kate, and I can't believe I'm saying this, we were trying to help *you*," Gordo said.

Kate looked at them, utterly surprised.

"Why would you guys want to help me?"

"Because everybody needs a friend," Lizzie told her.

"And you obviously don't have any," Miranda added.

"And we don't want to be 'em," Gordo said to make this perfectly clear. "So we have to get your old ones back."

Kate shook her head. "There's nothing you can do to help me," she said hopelessly.

"Think," Lizzie told her. "There's gotta be something."

"I can't be a cheerleader with my arm in a sling," Kate whined. "You can't do any stunts with one arm."

That was it! A huge lightbulb flicked on in Lizzie's head. "There's tons of stunts you can do with one arm," Lizzie said excitedly. Plan B was here!

"Like what?" Kate looked doubtful.

"Cartwheels, round-offs . . . tons of stuff. When I was doing rhythmic gymnastics, most of the stunts were one-handed," Lizzie explained.

Miranda's eyes opened wide. "Lizzie, that's it!" she cried.

Gordo turned to Kate. "What are you doing after school today?" he asked, ready to get the plan in motion.

Kate made a face. "Gordo, I may not be popular anymore, but I'm not that desperate."

Miranda rolled her eyes. "No," she said slowly. "Lizzie is going to train you to do one-armed stunts." Gordo shared a look with Miranda—the sooner they got Kate out of their hair, the better.

Kate's face softened. She looked at Lizzie. "You're going to teach me? You would do that for me?" she asked quietly.

Awww, look at her. She's harmless.

Lizzie smiled. "Sure. It's totally easy. You'll get the hang of it in no time."

"And we get to put Claire in her place," Miranda added. "What a witch!" Kate looked at her. Miranda shrugged. "Like you weren't thinking it," she said.

CHAPTER SEVEN

After school that afternoon, Mr. and Mrs. McGuire stood before the closed door of Matt's bedroom. On the other side of the door, they could hear Matt practicing his line for the school play.

"*Ah!* The doorbell! I'll *get* that!" Matt exclaimed. And then, in a lower voice, "Ah! The *door*bell! *I'll* get that!"

"Are you sure he needs a talking-to?" Mr.

McGuire asked his wife. "Maybe he's just excited about the play."

Just then, they heard Matt say, "Mirror, mirror on the wall, who's the greatest actor of them all?"

Mrs. McGuire looked at her husband and raised her eyebrows. He nodded. They knew what they had to do.

"After you," he said, opening the door. Together, they walked into the bedroom. Matt was standing before a full-length mirror, admiring his face from different angles.

"Matt, we need to talk to you," Mr. McGuire said.

"I'm busy," Matt said, without looking away from the mirror. "I can fit you in later."

Mrs. McGuire scowled. "We're your parents," she said sternly. "We don't make appointments."

Matt sighed, and turned to face them. "Fine, I'll practice later."

"That's what we want to talk to you about," his mother said. "This part . . . well, it's going to your head."

"My head?" Matt cried, placing a hand to his chin. "This head is . . . perfect! I mean, look at this face!" He grinned at his parents, then turned to admire his smile in the mirror. "Ah! The doorbell! I'll get that!" he said to his reflection.

Mr. McGuire frowned. "What we're trying to say, Matthew, is that just because you're in a play, it doesn't give you the right to order people around," he said. "Like your mother. And your friends."

"I don't order them around," Matt said. His parents looked at him skeptically. "I just tell them what to do," Matt admitted. "Isn't that what actors do?"

"No. Actors *act*," his mother told him. "Prima donnas order people around."

"So, here's what we're going to do," Mr. McGuire said. "You can be in the play. And we'll come watch . . ."

"But when we come home, you're grounded for a week," Mrs. McGuire finished. "You can use the time to think about how you've treated other people."

"How can you do this?" Matt cried. "The day before my play? You're just jealous! You're all jealous! I don't even want you guys to come to my play and hear me say—" Suddenly his voice broke off. *"Ah! The doorbell. I'll get that,"* Matt croaked in a hoarse whisper.

He clutched his throat with one hand, his eyes widening in alarm. *"Mom? Dad?"*

"He's getting pretty good at this acting thing," Mr. McGuire whispered to his wife.

She shook her head. It seemed as if Matt really *was* losing his voice!

"My voice! I'm ruined. I can't go on," Matt rasped.

His mother looked at him for a moment, as if considering something. "You know what?" she said finally. "Forget about being grounded. Losing your voice is punishment enough." She turned to leave.

"*Wait!*" Matt gasped. He slumped onto his bed, still clutching his throat dramatically.

Meanwhile, out in the McGuires' backyard, Lizzie and her friends were putting Operation Re-popularize Kate into action. Kate, Miranda, and Gordo watched from the edge of the porch as Lizzie demonstrated a perfect one-handed cartwheel. When she had finished, Miranda and Gordo clapped and whistled.

"Your turn," Lizzie told her.

Nervously, Kate rose and walked over to the lawn. Raising her right arm above her head, she took a few running steps. But at the edge of the mat she stopped short and lowered her arm. "I can't do it," she said to Lizzie. She was terrified of hurting herself again.

Lizzie figured what Kate needed was the support of friends. Anyone's friends. She turned to Miranda and Gordo. "Come on, guys," she said. "I need your help."

With Miranda and Gordo standing on either side, ready to catch her if she fell, Lizzie coached Kate through a one-handed cartwheel. Taking a few cautious steps, Kate planted her good hand on the mat, kicked up her legs, and—ta-da! Her feet flipped over her head. Right side up, she brushed her long hair away from her face and grinned at Lizzie in amazement. "I did it!" she cried.

Lizzie grinned back. "I told you it was easy."

By dinnertime, Lizzie had taught Kate how to do one-handed cartwheels, round-offs, and even front walk-overs. Miranda and Gordo clapped and whistled as Lizzie and Kate did a row of perfect one-handed cartwheels side by side on the mat. When they reached the end of the mat, Kate beamed proudly and slapped hands with Lizzie.

"I can't wait to go to school tomorrow and show Claire up," Kate said, collecting her things to go home.

Lizzie waited for a thank-you but when none came, her smile faded. "You're *welcome*, Kate," Lizzie finally said, miffed. She couldn't believe Kate could go right back to acting superior. As if nothing had happened.

Kate glanced at her. "Thanks," she said begrudgingly. "But you know this doesn't change anything. It's not like we're all suddenly going to be friends." She picked up her backpack and swung it onto her shoulder. "I'll see you guys tomorrow." She ran her fingers through her long hair and turned to leave.

Looks like my bunny grew some fangs.

Lizzie folded her arms across her chest. "Bye."

"See ya," Gordo told Kate.

"Later," Miranda said flatly, as Kate flounced out of the yard.

Lizzie and her friends glanced at one another. "I can't believe her," Gordo said.

"Why do we even bother?" Miranda asked.

Lizzie wondered the same thing. But then she decided she wasn't going to regret doing something nice, even if it was for someone who wasn't very nice.

"Guys, we did it because she was miserable," Lizzie reminded them. "And life with Claire was unbearable. Think about it. Did we really want to be friends with Kate?"

"Good point," Miranda said.

Gordo sat back down on the edge of the porch. "Just once I'd like to hear Kate Sanders say 'thank you' and mean it," he said. Lizzie and Miranda nodded.

Just then, Kate reappeared around the corner of the house. "Gordo?" she said.

Gordo sat up in surprise. "Yeah?"

Kate pointed at the porch. "You're sitting on my sweater."

"Oh." Gordo's face fell. He pulled Kate's brown sweater from beneath him and tossed it to her. She caught it with one hand and walked off without another word.

Lizzie and Miranda couldn't help but laugh.

"I think we'll be waiting for quite a while," Lizzie said.

CHAPTER EIGHT

The next day, Matt's throat was so sore, he had to stay home from school. He lay in bed thinking about the school play. How could it go on? Without someone to say his line, the whole play would fall apart!

As Matt fretted, the door to his room suddenly opened. Mrs. McGuire entered, carrying a tray with a steaming bowl of soup on it.

"Here, honey, this should make your throat

feel better," she said gently. "And I removed the carrots—just how you like it."

"Thanks," Matt whispered hoarsely. He looked at the soup. It was chicken noodle, his favorite kind. But he didn't feel very hungry. Something was still bothering him. "Mom, I'm really sorry about the way I acted. About the acting thing," he whispered.

His mother smiled and touched her finger to his lips. "Shh," she said. "Don't speak."

Matt smiled gratefully at his mother. He knew that was her way of telling him everything was okay. Suddenly, he felt ravenous. He picked up his spoon and was just about to take a sip of soup, when the doorbell rang.

"Ah!" Mrs. McGuire said, her eyes twinkling mischievously. "The doorbell! I'll get that!" Matt winced. Mothers!

A few moments later, the door to Matt's room opened again and Lanny walked in. He came over to the side of the bed and gazed at Matt, his eyes filled with concern.

"No, Lanny," Matt whispered. "I was a jerk for making you do all of those things for me."

Lanny pursed his lips and nodded.

"I'm sorry, Lanny. You're right. I let it all go to my head," Matt said sincerely. "But now I can barely speak."

Lanny raised his fist and tapped it twice again his own chest, sympathetically.

Matt shook his head. "No, Lanny, you have no idea what it feels like."

Lanny lifted his chin bravely.

"You'd do that for me?" Matt asked, sitting up in bed. "You'd perform in my place?"

Lanny smiled and nodded.

"Thanks, Lanny," Matt murmured, then added, "break a leg."

As Lanny left, Matt settled back down

under the covers, relieved to know that the show would go on.

At that moment, over at the junior high, Lizzie, Miranda, and Gordo were sitting in the back row of bleachers in the gymnauseum watching cheerleading practice. On the gym floor, Claire bossed the other cheerleaders through a new routine. Fifteen minutes into practice, Kate still hadn't arrived.

"Do you think she'll show?" Miranda asked, anxious for the real show to start.

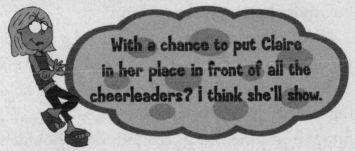

With a chance to put Claire in her place in front of all the cheerleaders? I think she'll show.

"She'd better show after all that time we spent with her," Lizzie answered.

"Can I remind you guys that we're here to support a girl who told us that she would never be friends with us—ever?" Gordo asked.

"But she's still better than Claire," Miranda said.

As they watched, Claire set down her pompoms and turned a perfect cartwheel. Lizzie wondered if Claire would even be impressed with Kate's one-armed tricks. "What if this doesn't work out?" she asked.

"It's gotta work," Gordo replied. "I can't eat one more lunch on the ground."

"We'll know soon enough," Lizzie said, pointing to the door. "Kate's here."

Kate strode into the gym, her chin held high. Her left arm, wrapped in a bandage, still hung from the sling around her shoulder. Ignoring the surprised looks of the other cheerleaders, she walked straight up to Claire.

Claire placed her hands on her hips. "Um, this is *cheerleading* practice?" she said frostily. "And you're no longer a cheerleader."

"Ooooh, what?" Kate asked, her eyes widening in mock horror. "Is the new cheerleading captain afraid of a little competition?"

"Competition?" Claire laughed. "Anything you can do, I can do better." She folded her arms and tilted her chin challengingly. "Bring it on."

Kate smiled. This is what she'd been waiting for. Slowly, she walked over to the exercise mats. Turning to face the room, she raised her right arm above her head. She took two steps, then dove forward into a one-handed front walk-over, followed quickly by two cartwheels. Her legs were perfectly straight, toes pointed like a ballerina. Spinning on her heel, she did another one-handed cartwheel and a round-off back to the corner where she'd started. But Kate wasn't done yet. She paused for a moment to focus. Then, taking a few running steps, she suddenly flipped over in an aerial cartwheel—*using no hands at all!*

The cheerleaders gasped. Claire's eyes bugged out in astonishment. Lizzie, Miranda, and Gordo rose to their feet, clapping and whistling. The aerial was the hardest stunt Lizzie had taught Kate, but Kate landed it perfectly. Grinning, Kate brushed the hair from her face. Then she whipped around to face Claire.

"Your turn," she said.

Claire licked her lips nervously and glanced over at the other cheerleaders. They stared back at her, waiting to see what she would do. Trying to regain her composure, Claire smiled smugly at Kate, then walked over to the corner of the mat. She took a deep breath and raised her arms. The room was so silent, you could have heard a pom-pom drop.

Claire took a running start into a round-off.

But as she landed, her foot twisted beneath her. She stumbled and fell, sprawling full-length onto the mats.

"Aaaaah!" she cried.

Everyone stared at her silently. When Claire rose to her feet, she was clutching her wrist. She shuffled over to the cheerleaders. "Guys? I think I hurt my wrist," she whimpered.

Kate looked at Claire's wrist, which was already starting to swell. "That doesn't look good," she said coldly. "I guess you can't be a cheerleader with a bad wrist. Which means you can't be cheerleading captain." Without another word, she turned to the other cheerleaders. "Ready! Let's go!" she called. With Kate in the lead, they began to practice another routine, leaving Claire standing alone.

In the bleachers, Gordo looked at Lizzie and Miranda. "I can't believe we helped Kate," he said.

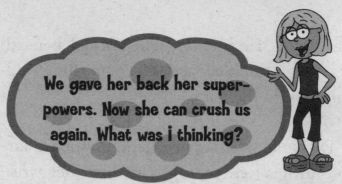

We gave her back her super-powers. Now she can crush us again. What was I thinking?

"Great idea, Lizzie," Miranda said, shaking her head in disbelief.

"I just can't believe that she didn't learn anything from the whole thing," Lizzie said as they climbed down the bleachers. "She treats people like dirt. They treated her like dirt, and now she treats them like dirt again."

Miranda shrugged. "It's the circle of life."

"And so the natural order of things has been restored," Gordo said.

Lizzie laughed. She put her arms around Gordo and Miranda's shoulders, and, as Kate and the rest of the squad continued to cheer, the three friends headed for home.

CHAPTER NINE

The next day at lunch, Lizzie, Miranda, and Gordo sat at a table in the quad, happily munching slices of pizza. Order had been restored to Hillridge Junior High. Now that Kate was head cheerleader again, kids were free to walk down all the hallways, use all the bathrooms, and sit anywhere they wanted in the quad. *Except* the cheerleaders' table, of course. From where she was sitting, Lizzie could see Kate in her usual spot at the head of the table. She was smiling and talking with the other cheerleaders.

At that moment, Claire entered the quad, carrying her lunch tray with one hand. Her right arm hung in a sling. Lizzie, Miranda, and Gordo watched as she shuffled past them, looking at the ground.

"Looks like Claire sprained her wrist," Lizzie said.

"If you have any great ideas about helping Claire, count me out," said Miranda.

Lizzie shook her head. "I'm just happy to be out of that hallway," she said with relief.

They watched as Claire walked over to a corner of the quad and sat down alone at a table. A moment later, Kate stood up. She walked over to Claire.

"Here we go," said Miranda. "So what do you think she's gonna do for revenge? Pudding as a hat? Applesauce down the shirt?"

i'll take humiliation in front of the whole school for $500. Alex.

"It's never going to change," Lizzie said, finally feeling defeated by all the meanness. "I don't even know why I bothered."

"Because you're a good person, Lizzie," Gordo said reassuringly, putting his arm across her shoulder.

They watched as Kate said something to Claire. Then she picked up Claire's tray and carried it back to the cheerleaders' table. Claire rose from her seat and followed her.

Lizzie stared in disbelief. "What's she doing?" she asked.

Miranda frowned. "You don't think—"

"It couldn't be," said Gordo.

But sure enough, Kate and Claire sat down

next to each other at the cheerleading table. Kate whispered something to Claire, and they laughed together.

"I can't believe it. Kate actually learned how to be a decent friend," Lizzie said in amazement.

Just then, Kate looked up and saw Lizzie watching her. The two girls locked eyes for a moment; then Kate smiled a genuine smile. Lizzie smiled warmly back at her. For a second, it seemed that Kate really *had* transformed into a decent friend.

But just then, Claire glanced up to see what Kate was looking at. When she saw Lizzie, she wrinkled her nose, making a face as if to say, "What*ever*." Immediately, Kate stopped smiling and made a face at Lizzie, too. She went back to talking with Claire.

Lizzie rolled her eyes and shook her head. Some things would *never* change.

PART
TWO

CHAPTER ONE

"**D**on't you love fall?" Lizzie asked Miranda and Gordo one early autumn morning as they kicked through a pile of leaves on the lawn of Hillridge Junior High. Lizzie took a deep breath of the crisp September air. "Leaves turning colors, ducks flying south . . ."

"The return of corduroy," Miranda added, gesturing to her stylin' new red corduroy hip huggers.

"The cycles of life reminding us that

everything must change—" Gordo broke off abruptly at the sight of Kate Sanders. She was heading straight for Lizzie and her friends, and she was leading a small parade. Marching behind Kate was the entire cheerleading squad, followed by a group of eighth-grade boys. As usual, Kate was dressed in her "adult" clothes—a blue turtleneck minidress—with her long, blond hair carefully curled and pinned up in a barrette. Everyone else had on black-and-white T-shirts with THE KATE/THE PARTY printed across the chest.

"Here's Lizzie and her little friends Whoever and Whatever," Kate said, flipping her hands indifferently at Miranda and Gordo.

"And some things will never change. . . ." Gordo said, gesturing to the always insulting pom-pom queen.

"My mom is making me invite the whole class to my birthday party. Losers, too," Kate informed Lizzie and her friends, so they didn't get the wrong idea. She snapped her fingers over her shoulder. "Hit it," she told the three boys behind her.

Suddenly, the boys burst into an a cappella harmony. *"Kate will see you at the door. Kate will free you, have some more . . .*

"Birthday cake and hit the dance . . .

"Floor."

Lizzie, Miranda, and Gordo couldn't believe what they were witnessing. A singing party invitation? Who does that?

"R.S.V.P.! R.S.V.P.!" the boys sang. *"It's gonna be* off the heazeee!" Putting their heads close together, two of the boys began to chant, *"The Kate, The Kate, The Kate, The Kate . . ."* while the other boy sang, *"The Party, The Party, The Party, The Pa-ar-ty. . . ."*

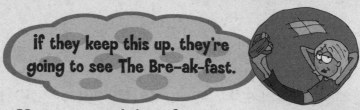

if they keep this up, they're going to see The Bre-ak-fast.

Kate snapped her fingers again, and the boys stopped. The cheerleaders pulled colorful, sparkly invitation cards from baskets on their arms and tossed them casually at Lizzie and her friends. Then Kate and her group moved on.

Miranda looked down at the card in her hand. "She's turning fourteen?" she asked.

"For the second year in a row, or is it the third?" Lizzie asked.

"She has a driver's license. I've seen it," Miranda informed them.

Lizzie's eyes opened wide. "Really?"

"No." Miranda smirked. "But it's a really good rumor to start, huh?"

As they turned to head into the school, a group of kids walked by, waving their invitations and chanting, "*The Kate. The Party. The Kate. The Party. . . .*"

Lizzie and her friends stopped to watch them pass. "Impressive," said Gordo sarcastically. "She's got the whole school chanting her name."

Lizzie held up her invitation to rip it in half. "I wouldn't go to this party if it were the last party . . ." she started to say.

Just then, they passed two boys holding invitations. "Last year, she gave out cell phones in the goody bags," one of the boys said. Lizzie looked at him, looked at her invitation, then looked at Miranda and Gordo and grinned. "I'm there," she said.

"Me, too," said Miranda.

Gordo leaned over to the boy and asked, "Did that include long-distance?"

The boy shrugged, as if it were obvious. "Duh," he said.

CHAPTER TWO

"**M**om, be reasonable!" Lizzie cried. "Can't we talk about this?"

Lizzie and her mother were standing in the kitchen, making dinner. Lizzie had casually mentioned Kate's party to her mother when she'd gotten home from school that afternoon. Little had she known that it was going to turn into a two-hour battle with her mother, Mrs. Strictness. Mrs. No Fun McGuire.

"Talk away," Mrs. McGuire said calmly,

"but you're not going to a party where there's no chaperone."

"I repeat for the nine hundredth time—there *will* be a chaperone," Lizzie said.

"And for the nine hundredth time, Kate's eighteen-year-old cousin, Amy, who 'plays in a band,' doesn't count," Mrs. McGuire told her firmly.

"Why not? Kate's mom thinks it's okay," Lizzie pointed out.

"Kate's mom and I have very different ideas of what's appropriate," Mrs. McGuire replied, pulling a package of tomatoes out of the refrigerator.

"That's because she *trusts* Kate," Lizzie snapped at her mother's back.

Mrs. McGuire whirled around. "Elizabeth Brooke McGuire, that tone of voice has 'grounded' written all over it," she said, pointing a warning finger.

Maintain, McGuire. Calmly explain to her how important this is to you.

"But, Mom, everybody's going to be there," Lizzie whined in a last-ditch attempt.

"Everybody except an appropriate chaperone. And you," her mother replied sternly. She smiled at Lizzie. "Honey, why are you in such a hurry to grow up?" she asked gently. "Just enjoy being a kid."

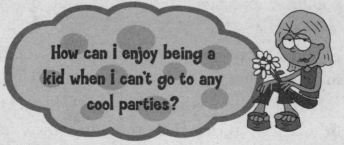

How can i enjoy being a kid when i can't go to any cool parties?

Suddenly, the front door slammed. From the front hallway, Matt shouted, "Mom!

Mom! We're going to be on TV!" He ran into the kitchen, followed by Mr. McGuire.

Lizzie folded her arms at the sight of her spastic little brother. "Is there going to be a new reality show?" she asked. *"Real Stories of the Really Clueless?"*

"You know, that was actually very, very clever. When I'm a big star, maybe you can write for me," Matt said sarcastically.

"That'd be great," Lizzie said sarcastically. "But I won't be able to go with you to any cool premiere parties, because they won't be *chaperoned.*" She glared at her mother one last time, then turned on her heel and stomped out of the room.

Mr. McGuire looked at his wife and raised his eyebrows. What was that all about? She shook her head and smiled. "Once again, I am the Worst Mother in the World," she told him.

"Cool, because I've just been out being Fun Dad," Mr. McGuire replied.

"Only the funniest," Matt told his mother. "You're looking at the next spokes-family for Cardio Punch Sports Drink."

"This casting lady in the mall picked us to be in a commercial," Mr. McGuire explained.

Mrs. McGuire's eyes brightened. "Oh! Spokes-family? Where do we go?" she asked.

Matt and his father glanced at each other. "Actually," Matt said slowly, "when they said, 'Spokes-family,' what they meant was, Spokes-Dad and Spokes-Matt."

"Oh." Mrs. McGuire's face fell. "So they don't need a mom?"

"Sorry, it's a guy thing," Matt patted his mother's back consolingly and went off to the living room to watch TV.

"But you on *camera*?" Mrs. McGuire shook her head doubtfully, remembering their wedding day. "You forgot to say 'I do' when you saw Cousin Ree-Ree with the video camera," she reminded him.

"I didn't forget," Mr. McGuire said.

His wife folded her arms and cocked one eyebrow.

"I was blinded by your beauty," he said weakly.

"Oh, please," his wife said. "You flinched for your driver's license picture."

"Look, it's something Matt really wants to do," Mr. McGuire told her. "I can get over being a little camera-shy for one day. That's why I am the Fun Dad! Whoo-hoo! Whoo-hoo!" Whooping it up, Mr. McGuire headed off to the living room to watch TV with Matt. Mrs. McGuire pursed her lips with annoyance. Just once, she'd like to be the fun parent.

The next day at school, Lizzie and her

friends compared notes on what their mothers had said about Kate's party.

"She started with my full name. She finished with 'Enjoy your childhood.' Fill in the blanks," Lizzie reported as they walked into the quad during the break.

"My mom gave me, 'I don't agree with Kate's mom on how to raise children,'" Miranda said, throwing her hands into the air in exasperation. "'Raise!' Like we're chickens or something!"

Gordo coolly tipped back his head and drained the last of his soda from its can. "My mom said it was okay."

"*What?*" Lizzie and Miranda whipped their heads around to stare at him.

"It's kinda depressing, really," Gordo said, perching on the edge of a table. "Do they think I'm such a good kid that I can never get into trouble?"

"Yes," Miranda said.

"I can *make* trouble," Gordo told them. "I've got a dark side. I can disrespect the common areas. I can act without regard for the safety of others!" To make his point, he held up his soda can and casually flung it over his shoulder.

The can flew through the air and hit a boy standing across the quad. "Ow!" the boy yelped, rubbing his head.

Gordo gasped and spun around. "I'm so sorry!" he called. He glanced back at Miranda and Lizzie, then added, "Sorry, but *bad*." Turning back to the boy, he cried, "Can I get you a towel?" He snatched up a napkin from the table and scurried over to help him.

As the student fended off Gordo's attempts to dab soda off his head, Lizzie turned back to Miranda. "I'm not giving up on this," she said. "We need to go to that party. Everybody's going to be there."

The two girls stared at each other in silence. "Why should we have to suffer to exercise our constitutional right to the pursuit of happiness?" Lizzie said at last. "It's positively un-American!"

Miranda looked at her thoughtfully. "How about this? Instead of *not* going to the party, we just . . . *go*," she said.

Lizzie frowned, confused. "But our parents already said we couldn't."

"We . . . do it, anyway," Miranda explained. "We just don't tell them."

Lizzie stared at her friend for a moment, surprised.

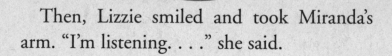

This sounds like it involves a little bit of lying and deception, but a whole lotta going to the party.

Then, Lizzie smiled and took Miranda's arm. "I'm listening. . . ." she said.

CHAPTER THREE

On Friday afternoon, Mr. McGuire picked Matt up from school, and the two of them drove across town to the television studio where the Cardio Punch commercial would be filmed. As they walked through the door of the soundstage, Matt gripped his father's hand with excitement.

"Dad, here we are. The doorway *to stardom!*" he cried, raising his fist in the air.

Mr. McGuire looked around nervously.

The soundstage was a huge, warehouselike room, filled with equipment and props. Young men and women wearing headsets and carrying clipboards bustled back and forth. Over to the side of the room, Mr. McGuire noticed a large piece of equipment that looked like it might be a TV camera. He took a deep breath.

"Okay," he murmured to himself. "It's not going to be a big deal. I'm not going to be on camera for that long. This is just a fun day together, trying something new."

"Something new, *like stardom*!" Matt added, raising his fist again.

His father gave him a look. "Here, let's just sign in," he said, leading them over to a table with a sign-up sheet.

"On the sign-in sheet . . . *to stardom*!" Matt cried.

"Stop doing that!" Mr. McGuire told him,

grabbing Matt's raised hand and lowering it to his side.

"There they are!" a woman cried from across the room. Mr. McGuire and Matt looked up and saw a tall blond woman in a gray suit striding toward them. It was Donna, the casting woman who had spotted them in the mall. Next to her was a man with a Beatles-style haircut and long sideburns. Even though it was warm in the studio, he wore a heavy turtleneck sweater under his jacket. He made a square with both hands and peered through it at Matt and Mr. McGuire, as if framing them with a camera.

"It's the real father and his real little boy I found in the shoe store," Donna told the man. She turned to the McGuires. "This is Steve, our director!" she said brightly.

Matt beamed. "The man who will direct us to *star*—"

"Shush," Mr. McGuire said, cutting him off. He shook hands with the director. "Sam McGuire," he said, introducing himself. "This is my son, Matt."

"Hi," Matt said. He vigorously pumped the director's outstretched hand, grinning from ear to ear.

The director smiled. "Love them," he said to Donna. "Have the stunt guys fit them with harnesses." He nodded briefly at the McGuires, then shouted, "Robyn! Where's my blended?" A second later, a very hassled-looking assistant scurried up and handed him a coffee drink in a take-out cup.

Mr. McGuire leaned down to Matt. "Did he say '*harness*'?"

"The harness *to stardom*!" Matt replied happily.

Mr. McGuire glanced up and suddenly noticed a menacing twenty-foot rock-climbing wall towering above them. At the top of the wall, a man began to adjust the ropes attached to two harnesses. One of the harnesses was Matt-sized. The other looked like it was Dad-sized.

Mr. McGuire gulped. "I think I know what the harness is for," he said.

Matt stood next to him, staring at the wall with a dazed expression on his face. "This is the best day of my life," he murmured.

Mr. McGuire glanced nervously at his son. The last thing in the world he wanted to do was to climb that wall, but he didn't want to tell that to Matt. Instead, he said, "Matt, if this wall is too high for you, we don't have to do this."

"Too high?" Matt cried. "It's not high enough! Whoo-hoo!" He danced from side to side, shouting, "Who's your rock climber? Who's your rock climber?"

Suddenly, the director walked over to them. "Let's run over this," he said crisply. "You scale the wall, you grab the Cardio Punch. Chug and smile. Rappel back down one-handed with the bottle, label out, give me a flip at the end, touch down, and smile. Yes?"

Mr. McGuire stared at him. "This can't be safe," he said.

The director looked at him coolly. "If it isn't, we'll fix it in editing." He flashed a phony smile at Mr. McGuire, then bellowed, "Robyn?"

The harried assistant ran over with a sheaf of papers. "I need you to sign these waivers," she told Mr. McGuire, shoving a pen into his hand. "Sign here, here. . . ." She flipped to another page. "Initial here, and can I have your thumb . . . ?" Grabbing Mr. McGuire's thumb, she rolled it across an ink pad and stamped his thumbprint onto one of the pages.

"Let's make some magic, people! We're on a bell!" the director shouted.

Mr. McGuire turned pale.

Meanwhile, on the other side of town, in Lizzie's bedroom, Lizzie and Miranda were getting ready for their big performance— namely, convincing Lizzie's mom that they were going to the mall, when they were really headed for Kate's party. Although Lizzie's hair was freshly washed and carefully curled, she wore old jeans, a T-shirt, and a denim jacket. As she and Miranda packed their party clothes into shopping bags, they went over the final details of their plan.

"I downloaded the bus map," Miranda said, handing a piece of paper to Lizzie. "The Number Twenty-three drops us two blocks from Kate's house."

Lizzie stared down at the bus map. Her

hands were shaking so hard, she could barely see it. "I'm having second and third and fourth thoughts about this whole thing," she told Miranda.

Miranda grabbed Lizzie's hands to steady them. "Lizzie, you can't fall apart at a time like this," she said.

"At a time like what?" Lizzie cried. "A time like the first time we tell our mothers we're going to the mall, and we sneak to a party instead? I'd say that's the perfect time to fall apart!"

"They'll never know," Miranda reassured her. "Mall, bus, party, bus, mall. The plan is flawless."

Suddenly, the door to Lizzie's room opened. The girls jumped. But it was only Gordo. He slipped into the room and closed the door tightly behind him.

"So what's the plan?" he asked in a hushed voice.

"*Your* plan is that your parents take you to the party that you're allowed to go to," Miranda told him, annoyed.

"Oh, but that's where you're wrong," Gordo said cleverly. "I told my parents I wasn't going to the party. In fact, they think I'm at Miranda's house. But I'm not. I'm here. You wanna know why?" He lowered his voice to a menacing whisper. "'Cause I'm bad."

Miranda and Lizzie rolled their eyes. "We'll see you at the party, Gordo," Miranda said.

Gordo shook his head. "You're not getting rid of me that fast. 'Cause I'm all about the plan tonight. And you wanna know why?"

"Yeah, Gordo. You're baaaad," Miranda said sarcastically.

Just then, there was a brief knock on Lizzie's door, and Mrs. McGuire entered. "You girls ready?" she asked. She glanced over at Gordo. "Oh, hi, Gordo," she said, surprised. "You're going shopping with the girls?"

"That's the plan," Gordo replied. Lizzie and Miranda scowled at him.

As Miranda and Gordo left the room, Mrs. McGuire stopped Lizzie. "Can I talk to you for a second?" she asked.

Lizzie's breath caught in her chest.

She knows! How does she always know?

"Uh, sure, Mom," Lizzie said, barely managing to choke out the words.

"I know you really wanted to go to the party tonight," her mother said. "And I'm sorry I had to say no. But I'm sure you'll have a good time with your friends at the mall." She reached into her wallet and pulled out a ten-dollar bill. Smiling warmly, she held it out to Lizzie. "Buy everyone a big cookie on me!"

Lizzie gulped. "Thanks, Mom," she said weakly.

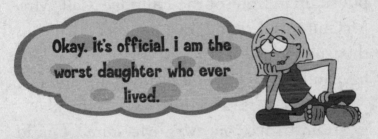

Stricken with guilt, Lizzie tucked the money into her pocket and followed her mother out to the car.

CHAPTER FOUR

At 6:30 P.M., the McGuires' station wagon pulled up in front of the Hillridge Mall. Mrs. McGuire smiled at Lizzie and her friends as they unbuckled their seat belts. "You kids have fun," she said. "I'll pick you up at ten."

"Thanks, Mrs. McGuire," said Miranda.

"Yeah, thank you, Mrs. McGuire," Gordo added.

Lizzie hesitated. She wondered if she should go through with it. Wasn't she a good girl? For an instant, she had the urge to stay in her seat until her mother turned the car around and drove her back home. But Miranda and Gordo were already climbing out of the car. It was too late to back out now.

Lizzie leaned over and kissed her mother on the cheek. "Thanks, Mom. See you tonight," she said. Taking a deep breath, she opened the door of the car and joined her friends on the sidewalk.

Inside the mall, Lizzie and Miranda headed straight for the women's rest room. While Gordo waited in the hallway, Lizzie and Miranda used the restroom stalls to change into their party clothes. Lizzie threw on a pink sequined top, black pants, and a knee-length black cardigan. Miranda slipped on sparkly black pants and a rust-colored vinyl jacket with a fake-fur collar.

Using the rest-room mirror, they brushed

mascara onto their eyelashes and dabbed on lip gloss. Checking herself in the mirror, Lizzie looked like a girl ready to party. She still felt guilty, but at least she *looked* like she was ready to have some fun.

After about 20 long minutes of waiting, Gordo walked over and pounded his fist on the rest-room door. Instantly, it flew open, and out came a plump, middle-aged woman. She scowled at Gordo and flicked him on the forehead with her index finger. Gordo turned bright red. Waiting for his friends was turning into risky business.

When at last they were ready, the three friends ran back through the mall, reaching the bus stop by 6:58, just as the bus was pulling up. On the five-minute ride to Kate's house, Lizzie imagined that she saw her mother's station wagon driving past on the street. She was having a major guilt attack.

By 7:03, they'd reached Kate's house, and Lizzie had a meltdown. "She gives me ten dollars!" she cried, as they walked up to the door. "I lied to my mother, and what does she do? She gives me ten dollars."

"Can you please save the guilt thing until *after* the party?" Miranda asked. "Trust me, knowing you, it will still be there."

"Not with me," Gordo said, pointing a thumb at his chest. "Guilt-free Gordo. You know why? *'Cause I'm baaaad*," he whispered.

Lizzie frowned. "No, 'cause you're . . . *allowed to be here*," she whispered back. But Miranda was right, she thought. She could feel guilty later—it was time to have some fun. She shook her hair away from her face, turned, and coolly pushed open the door.

A wave of noise washed over them. Kate's living room was packed with strangers—and everyone looked way older, like they were in high school or even college. Guys in baggy clothes and girls wearing spiky jewelry were moshing in the middle of the room. Over in the corner, a DJ the size of a professional football player was nodding his head along to the beat. Someone had pulled all the cushions off the couch, and now they were batting them around like beach balls.

Lizzie, Miranda, and Gordo stared at the scene in total disbelief. "Who *are* all these people?" Lizzie cried.

Before Miranda could answer, Lizzie was suddenly lifted off her feet. She screamed as two guys carried her into the middle of the living room. Next thing she knew, Lizzie was flat on her back, being passed over the top of the mosh pit like one of the sofa cushions!

"HELLLLP!" she screamed.

"Lizzie! Hang on!" Miranda cried.

Miranda and Gordo watched Lizzie get tossed over the crowd a couple more times. Then, suddenly, she disappeared from view. She'd been sucked into the mosh pit!

Miranda and Gordo ducked this way and that, trying to see around the flailing bodies. At last, they caught a glimpse of pink sequins. Lizzie's blond head bobbed up from the crowd.

"Lizzie! Hang on! Just go with it!" Gordo called.

But Lizzie screamed, so Miranda cried, "Give me your hand!" She and Gordo stuck their hands into the pit, and Lizzie grabbed hold. They pulled, using all their might. Finally, Lizzie popped out of the crowd like a cork out of a bottle. They hustled over to the wall of the living room and huddled against it for safety.

"What is going on here?" Lizzie asked.

"Total chaos," said Gordo.

And they still hadn't seen Kate or anyone from school. "Let's ditch our coats and see if we can find anyone we know," Miranda suggested. Lizzie and Gordo nodded. Together they made their way over to a hallway closet. A sign taped to the door said SEVEN MINUTES IN HEAVEN in orange crayon. Lizzie opened the door, flipped on a light . . . and gasped.

Kate's cousin Amy and a college-age guy were standing between the coats, kissing. When the light went on, Amy looked up. Her curly blond hair was all messed up, and her lipstick was smeared. She glared at Lizzie, Miranda, and Gordo.

"Wait your turn," she snapped.

"Sorry, sorry," Lizzie said, nervously turning off the light and pulling the door closed. She looked at her friends helplessly.

Gordo pointed to the closet and frowned. "I think that was our chaperone," he said.

CHAPTER FIVE

Lizzie, Miranda, and Gordo huddled together in the coat closet. They'd circled the party twice, but this was the only place they could find that was safe and quiet enough to talk.

"I thought the whole class was coming. Do you see anybody you know?" Gordo asked.

"I don't think so," Miranda replied. "Nobody in our homeroom has a beard."

"I guess their parents wouldn't let them come, either," Lizzie said.

Gordo shook his head. "This is bad. New plan. I say we go back to the mall, split a giant cookie, and call it a night."

"I'm there," Lizzie said.

"*Vamanos,*" said Miranda.

"On my count," Gordo said. "One, two . . ."

Suddenly, the door opened. "Aaaah!" Lizzie and her friends fell back, shrieking. Kate stood before them, hands on her hips.

"Your seven minutes was up ten minutes ago," she said as she tapped her watch.

"Don't worry, Kate. We were just leaving, anyway," Miranda told her.

Lizzie dug through her purse and pulled out a small, gift-wrapped box. "Happy birthday," she said, handing the box to Kate. "We had a lovely time. Thank you for inviting us." She started to edge toward the door.

But Kate blocked her path. She was trying to think of a way to get Lizzie and her friends to stay, without sounding like she wanted them to stay. "I can't believe you guys are leaving before all the cool people get here," she tried.

Gordo shrugged. "That's us. Big fat losers. Bye." Together, Gordo, Lizzie, and Miranda stepped toward the door.

"Wait!" Kate held up her hands, blocking their way again. "We're about to cut the cake."

"There's cake?" Gordo's eyes widened. He grabbed Lizzie and Miranda and pulled them back. "You guys! There's cake!" Lizzie and Miranda rolled their eyes. Gordo wasn't allowed sweets at home. His parents thought sugar was *baaad*.

Just then, Amy walked over, wheeling a huge cake on a serving cart. Kate looked down at the cake, which was covered with creamy white frosting and strawberries.

"You said you wanted chocolate, right?" Amy asked her.

Kate stared at the cake, which was clearly not chocolate. "Right."

"Phew!" Amy sighed with relief. "I got strawberry. I like it better. I'm just glad I remembered what you wanted."

Kate's brow wrinkled. This party was getting worse by the minute. "And where are the candles?" she snapped.

Amy held up her hands defensively. "I was just told cake. Nobody said anything about candles," she said.

"But it's my birthday," Kate said.

"Oh, it is?" Amy looked at her, genuinely surprised. "Happy birthday."

Lizzie, Miranda, and Gordo gaped at Amy. How could she have not known it was Kate's birthday? Oblivious to Kate's disappointment, Amy wheeled the cake over to the living room. All of a sudden, Kate saw a crowd of hungry people reaching for her birthday cake. "Wait!" she cried, running into the living room. "Don't eat my cake! You haven't even sung me 'Happy Birthday'—" Kate wedged herself in front of the crowd, trying to hold them back. But a group of rowdy guys shoved forward and pushed Kate . . . face first into her cake!

When Kate stood up, her face was completely covered in frosting. She wiped her eyes, crying, "Stop! This isn't happening!"

Lizzie, Miranda, and Gordo stood frozen in their spots. "She's right," said Miranda. "I'm glad we didn't leave."

Amy tried to dab at Kate with a pink paper napkin, but Kate pushed her hand away. "No! Move! Get away from me, you snakes!" she cried, her eyes filling with tears of embarrassment. She shoved through the crowd and ran from the room. As soon as she was gone, the crowd closed in on the cake.

"Harsh," said Gordo.

it's hard to tell through the frosting, but Kate does look upset.

"Nobody deserves that on their birthday," Lizzie said. "I'm going to see if she's okay." Lizzie ran after Kate, leaving Miranda and Gordo standing in the living room. Gordo hungrily eyed the cake.

CHAPTER SIX

"**A**nd action!"

Steve the director and his entire crew stared up at the rock-climbing wall, where Matt and Mr. McGuire were hanging from their harness.

"I said, *action!*" Steve shouted a little louder, beginning to get frustrated. But Mr. McGuire stayed put, clinging to the wall for dear life.

"Action! That means move!" Matt told his father.

"I can't move," Mr. McGuire said through clenched teeth.

"Sure you can!" Matt said cheerfully. "See?" He pushed away from the rock wall, swinging out on his rope, then coming around to Mr. McGuire's other side. "I'm out! I'm in! I'm out!" He swung back around to the place where he'd started.

"Not helping!" Mr. McGuire gasped. A trickle of sweat ran down his temple.

"Dad, what's wrong?" Matt asked.

"Bad rope-climbing incident," his father replied. The memory of climbing a rope in high-school gym class flashed through Mr. McGuire's mind. Even only two feet off the ground, he'd been terrified. He'd fallen off the rope, and the whole class had laughed at him.

But Matt was still confused. "What do you mean?" he asked his father.

"Too high!" Mr. McGuire said hoarsely.

His knuckles were white from gripping the rock wall.

"Action!" the director shouted impatiently from below.

"Dad, are you afraid of heights?" Matt asked.

"Uh-huh." Mr. McGuire nodded.

Matt looked at him carefully. Now it all made sense. "Why didn't you say so?"

"I didn't want to let you down," Mr. McGuire told him.

On the ground, Steve folded his arms across his chest. "People, you're not making me happy!" he called. "One more time, chug and smile!"

Matt ignored the director. "Dad, you didn't have to do this for me," he said quietly.

"I know, but I wanted to," Mr. McGuire replied.

"Hey, you! Up there!" Steve hollered. "Are you scared or just stupid?"

Matt's face flushed with anger. He looked down at the director. "What did you say?" he asked slowly.

"I wasn't talking to you, kid. I was talking to that hundred and eighty pounds of useless fat hanging next to you," the director replied sharply.

Matt turned to his father. "I'll be back," he growled. Tightening the chin strap of his helmet, he flipped over and scaled down the wall, headfirst. When he reached the ground, he did a complete somersault, landing on his feet and pointing his fist at the director.

"Hey, buddy," Matt said furiously. "That's the best dad in the world hanging up there!" He jerked his thumb toward his father. "You're not good enough to point your little cameras at him! So, listen up. This is how it's gonna work. You're going to stop yelling at my dad, and I'll let you keep your kneecaps. Yes?"

The director stared at him in shock. "Yes," he replied meekly.

"Now, cut him loose, get me a blended, and that's a wrap!" Matt commanded.

For a moment the room was silent. Then, from the back of the room came the sound of someone clapping. Robyn, Steve's harried assistant, wiped a tear from her eye as she applauded Matt's performance. One by one, the rest of the crew began to clap, until the whole room was whistling and cheering. The crew lifted Matt onto their shoulders.

"Let's go get my dad!" Matt shouted, lifting his hands in the air triumphantly.

As Matt and the crew moved off to go help Mr. McGuire, Steve turned to the young woman who was operating the camera. "Did you get that?" he asked breathlessly.

The camera op grinned and held up her thumb, nodding "yes."

CHAPTER SEVEN

Lizzie walked slowly down the hallway to Kate's bedroom, the only part of the house that wasn't packed with partygoers. She was just about to knock on the door, when she overhead Kate say, "I know what time it is there, but this *is* a big thing, Mom."

Lizzie paused and peeped through the slightly open door. Kate was pacing back and forth, holding a cordless phone to her ear.

"Mom, they pushed me into my own cake,"

Kate cried into the phone. "They didn't even sing 'Happy Birthday.' She used my birthday party to invite her own friends." Kate paused, listening. Then she said, "Maybe if you were here, my friends would have been allowed to come! Mom, could you just come home, please . . . ? What . . . ? Mom, you're breaking up. Can you hear me?"

There was silence. Not sure exactly what to do, Lizzie waited until it was clear Kate had hung up the phone; then she knocked gently.

"Go away!" Kate yelled.

But Lizzie couldn't go away and leave Kate like this, so she stepped into the room. Kate was wiping frosting from her dress with a towel. "Are you okay?" Lizzie asked.

"Do I *look* okay?" Kate snapped.

"You look like you could use some help," Lizzie said.

"Wrong again, McGuire," Kate said rudely. "I don't need your help."

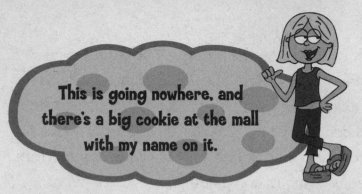

This is going nowhere, and there's a big cookie at the mall with my name on it.

Miranda and Gordo were right, Lizzie thought. Kate wasn't worth it. "Whatever," Lizzie snapped back at her. "Happy birthday. I'm out." She spun on her heel to leave.

But just then a loud crash came from the living room. Kate groaned. Lizzie turned back and saw Kate slumped on the bed, holding her head in her hands.

"Is this the party you wanted?" Lizzie asked gently.

"I wanted a few friends for movies," Kate told Lizzie sincerely. "But my mom said I should have a grown-up party instead. Then she left town." She sighed. "So I'm stuck here with one hundred of my cousin's closest friends."

"We came to see *you*, Kate," Lizzie told her.

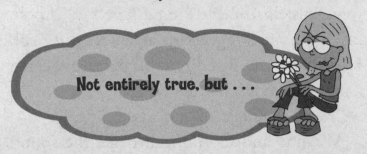

Not entirely true, but . . .

"Well, here I am," Kate said sadly. "You must love seeing me like this."

Oh, yeah!

"I do like seeing you like this. Like a normal person," Lizzie said. Kate gave her a small smile, then looked down at her hands.

At that moment, Miranda and Gordo came down the hall, munching slices of cake and looking for Lizzie. They arrived at Kate's room just in time to hear Lizzie say, "Look, my mom's picking us up at ten at the mall. How about you just ditch this party and catch a movie with a few friends?"

"Really?" Kate said, surprised.

Miranda and Gordo didn't like the sound of this—at all. They stared at Lizzie in horror.

"Sure," Lizzie told her. Then she stood up to leave and noticed Miranda and Gordo standing in the doorway looking stunned. "Oh, hi, guys," Lizzie said. "Kate is going with us."

"What are we going to see?" Kate asked excitedly as she followed Lizzie out of the room.

As soon as they were gone, Miranda turned to Gordo. "Oh, man! Kate Sanders coming with us was *not* part of the plan." Shaking their heads, they followed Lizzie and Kate.

In the living room, music blasted at full volume. People were still dancing around and on top of the furniture. A group played a game of tug-of-war with the living room curtains, while two guys in leather jackets and tinted glasses pretended to sword-fight with two of Mrs. Sanders's flowered umbrellas. A guy sitting on the couch unscrewed the top from a jar of mustard and poured the contents all over his shirt. Lizzie and her friends shuddered. *This* was a grown-up party?

Kate turned to them. "Lizzie, you guys go," she said. "I can't leave my house like this." Just then, she saw a tall guy pick up an expensive crystal egg from the mantelpiece. Grinning, he tossed the fragile object to his friend.

Kate almost fell over. It was her mother's crystal!

"Don't do that! Give me that!" Kate shrieked at him, elbowing her way through the crowd.

"I'm positive that helping Kate play keep-away with statues is not part of the plan," Gordo said. They watched as Kate wrestled the egg out of one of the guys' hands and returned it to the mantel.

"We can't leave her here like this," Lizzie said.

"She hates us," Miranda replied dryly. "We *can* leave her."

"I couldn't agree more," said Gordo. "And you want to know why? *Because I'm baaaad . . .* but this party is worse."

"You're right," Lizzie said. "What this party needs is a mom. So I'm calling mine."

"What?" Miranda gaped at her in horror. Obviously, her friend was losing it—fast. "Let's get that big cookie in you, quick! You're talking crazy!"

"No. It's the right thing to do," Lizzie said, her mind already made up.

"But we'll be so grounded," Miranda argued. "After all she's said and done to us, that would be so, so wrong."

"No, when our moms see how mature we've been, they'll be so proud of us, we'll be completely off the hook," Lizzie told her. She left her friends behind as she set off through the crowd in search of a phone.

Miranda and Gordo looked at each other. "That never works," Gordo said. "You think it's gonna, but then it doesn't."

Miranda shook her head. "We were so close," she said sadly.

CHAPTER EIGHT

Mrs. McGuire sat curled on the couch in the McGuires' living room, enjoying a quiet evening alone. An aromatherapy candle flickered softly on the coffee table, and a romantic movie played on the television. Mrs. McGuire sniffled as she spooned chocolate-chip ice cream straight from the carton. She was crying over a particularly sad part in the movie. She was just about to scoop up another spoonful of ice cream, when the phone rang.

"Hello?" she said brightly, trying to disguise the tears in her voice. She sat up when she heard Lizzie's voice at the other end of the line. "What? You need me? I'll be right there!" Slamming down the phone, Mrs. McGuire pulled on her coat and shoes and dashed out of the house.

Moments later, she arrived at the party. Squeezing in the door, Mrs. McGuire made her way through the packed living room, clutching her purse tightly against her body. At last, she spotted Lizzie, Miranda, and Gordo standing in a corner. "Kids, are you all right?" she asked, hurrying over to them.

"We're fine," Lizzie assured her.

"I'm glad you called me!" Mrs. McGuire shouted over the music.

Lizzie sighed with relief.

These are the times when i love
her so much.

"I know you said we shouldn't be here,"
Lizzie began. "And you were right about the
chaperone not being a chaperone."

Mrs. McGuire pursed her lips and nodded.

"And I totally learned my lesson, so you
don't need to punish me," Lizzie finished. She
smiled hopefully at her mother.

Mrs. McGuire laughed. "Ha-ha-ha. At least
you still have your sense of humor," she said.
"You're going to need it during your long,
lonely days of being grounded." Lizzie's face
fell. Mrs. McGuire turned and looked fondly
at her daughter's friends. "Ah, Miranda and
Gordo. I'll miss seeing you at the house."

"Uh, Mrs. McGuire. I'm actually allowed to be here," Gordo told her.

Mrs. McGuire smiled wryly at him. "Not when I'm done talking to your parents."

"That never works, either," Miranda muttered to Gordo.

"Mom, could you take all of *this* and move it *that* way?" Lizzie said, gesturing from the chaos in the living room to the open front door.

"Oh, sweetie, I'm just warming up," her mother replied cheerfully. "This will be fun."

And then there are times when she really, really scares me.

Squaring her shoulders, Mrs. McGuire

marched straight into the center of the crowd. Lizzie watched in amazement as her mother bustled around the room like a reverse hurricane, turning everything right side up. She pulled sandwiches from people's mouths and plastic cups from their hands, tossing them into large trash bags. She yanked the umbrellas away from the two guys, and scolded the people who were tugging at the curtains. Then, she stormed over to the corner where the DJ was playing, picked up the extension cord, and pulled the plug on the party.

The music came to an abrupt stop. Mrs. McGuire flicked on the lights. Blinking in the suddenly bright room, everyone turned to stare at her.

"Now hear this!" Mrs. McGuire bellowed like an army commander. "You don't have to go home, but you've got to get the heck out of here."

"Excuse me, uh, ma'am?" Amy said stepping up to Mrs. McGuire. "You're kind of, like, *stopping* the party."

"Exactly," Mrs. McGuire said confidently.

Amy flipped her blond curls, looking confused. "But that will, you know, stop the party," she said.

"Right," Mrs. McGuire said tersely.

"Hmm. So, the party will be over now?" Amy asked.

"Right now," Mrs. McGuire snapped.

"Oh." Amy placed her hands on her hips and arched her eyebrows. "And *you* are?"

"Me!" Mrs. McGuire stuck her face right up close to Amy's. Amy flinched. "I am your worst nightmare," Mrs. McGuire told her. "I'm a mother on a mission. And I hope you don't think I'm kidding." She turned to the crowd, and roared, "Now move, people!"

Everyone scurried toward the door. No

one wanted to mess with Mrs. McGuire.

"Buh-bye, now," Lizzie said as the people streamed past her.

"I'll just take that for you," Miranda said, pulling Mrs. Sanders's crystal egg from the hands of a departing guest. "Here," she said, passing the egg back to Kate.

"Buckle up for safety!" Gordo waved to the departing crowd.

When the house was finally empty, Mrs. McGuire patted Kate's arm. "You want to come home with us, sweetie?" she asked.

"I think I'm okay now," Kate replied. "Thanks so much, Mrs. McGuire."

Mrs. McGuire looked around at the trash that littered the living room and shook her head. "What a way to celebrate your fifteenth birthday," she said.

"Um, actually, it's my fourteenth," Kate told her.

Mrs. McGuire smiled knowingly. "Right," she said.

As Mrs. McGuire turned to leave, Lizzie walked up to Kate, looking for just a little gratitude herself. "Thanks, Lizzie?" she said, prompting her.

Kate looked at her reluctantly.

"I know. You'll deny you ever said it. Even under alien water torture," Lizzie said.

"Just so we're clear . . ." Kate began. Then she smiled sincerely. "Thanks, Lizzie."

Wow, that was a first. "Don't mention it," Lizzie said.

"Glad that's behind us," Kate sneered, and stalked off.

Lizzie rolled her eyes. After one brief shining moment, Kate was back to her old ways.

CHAPTER NINE

"So, this is being grounded, huh?" said Gordo, actually relishing his very first punishment.

Lizzie, Miranda, and Gordo sat on their beds in their own bedrooms, where they'd spent every moment of their free time for the past week. Fortunately, their parents hadn't taken away phone privileges, so at least they could commiserate on three-way phone calls.

"Yeah," Miranda replied. "It reeks."

"I'm *so* bored," Lizzie groaned, but she had to admit it felt good to be *gooooood.*

"I've actually gotten a lot of work done," Gordo said.

"Well, it's official. You're no longer 'bad,' Gordo," Miranda told him.

Just then, Lizzie's bedroom door opened. Mrs. McGuire poked her head into the room. "Lizzie, you can come downstairs," she said. "Matt and Dad's commercial is on."

"Gotta go," Lizzie told her friends. "More joy." Hanging up the phone, she headed downstairs and joined her family on the couch.

"Here it is! Here it is!" Mr. McGuire said, pointing to the TV with the remote control.

Rock music played in the background of the commercial as Matt crawled down the rock-climbing wall headfirst, flipped over, and faced a cartoon dragon. "Hey, buddy!

That's the best *punch* in the world up there!" he shouted at the dragon. He jerked his thumb over his shoulder at a giant bottle of Cardio Punch that was hanging over Mr. McGuire's place on the wall.

Watching, Mr. McGuire frowned. "I think that's me," he said.

"You're not good enough to pop the top on a bottle of that punch," on-screen Matt yelled at the cartoon dragon. "So, listen up. This is how it's gonna work. You're gonna stop hogging all the punch, and I'll let you keep your kneecaps. Yes?"

On the couch, Mr. McGuire turned and looked at Matt. "Hey, you never said any of that stuff," he said. The director had filmed Matt's angry speech and dubbed new words over the top! Matt thought it was inspired genius. He grinned as he watched himself get lifted onto the shoulders of the crew.

"Cardio Punch. The drink of spiky-headed tough kids everywhere," the commercial narrator said as the Cardio Punch logo appeared under Matt's face

On screen, Matt grinned and shouted, "Let's go get some punch!"

The commercial ended. Lizzie and her parents stared at the screen for a moment—then they politely clapped. It was certainly the strangest commercial they had ever seen.

Matt couldn't have been prouder. He smiled modestly and did a little bow. "Thank you," he said.

GET INSIDE HER HEAD

Lizzie McGuire

A Disney Channel Original Series

Weekends on **Disney CHANNEL** SM

Visit Lizzie @ ZoogDisney.com

© Disney